Grandpa I Just Wanna be a Cowboy:

Rodeo Cowboys

5/27/18

Books by Trae Q.L. Venerable

Grandpa I Just Wanna be a Cowboy: Notables from the West
Grandpa I Just Wanna be a Cowboy: Rodeo Cowboys
Grandpa I Just Wanna be a Cowboy: Women In the West

Grandpa I Just Wanna be a Cowboy:
Rodeo Cowboys

Trae Q.L. Venerable

SPEAKING VOLUMES, LLC
NAPLES, FLORIDA
2018

Grandpa I Just Wanna be a Cowboy:
Rodeo Cowboys

ISBN 978-1-62815-713-0

History has defined us for a long time.
But now, the truth about the
forgotten cowboys will come to the
light.

For all of the forgotten cowboys...
- Trae Q. L. Venerable

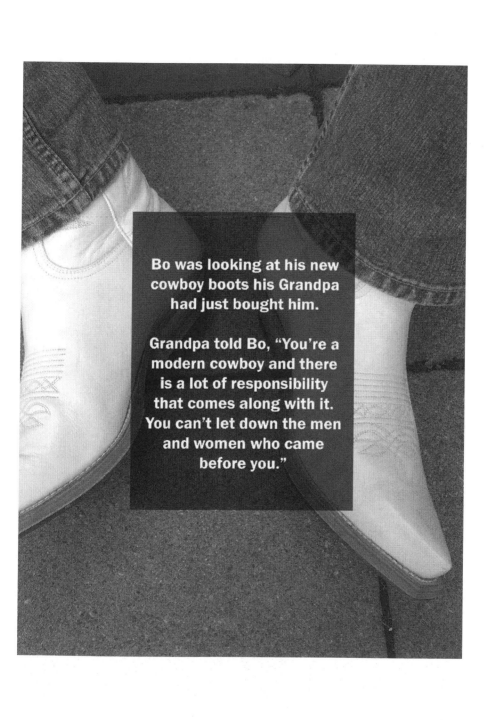

Bo was looking at his new cowboy boots his Grandpa had just bought him.

Grandpa told Bo, "You're a modern cowboy and there is a lot of responsibility that comes along with it. You can't let down the men and women who came before you."

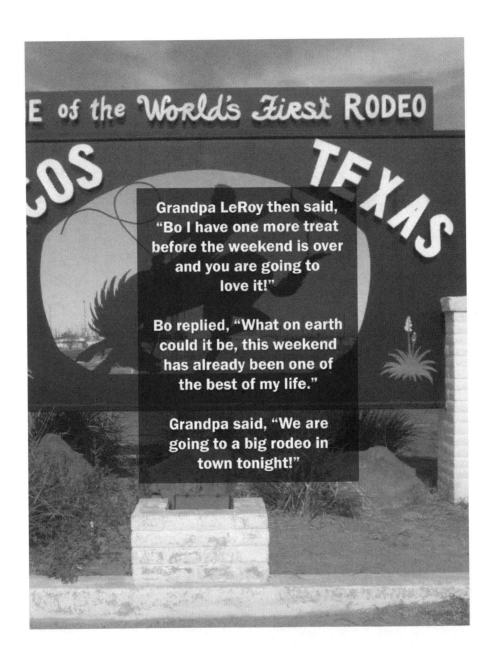

Now Bo was anxious to get to the rodeo tonight and watch his favorite Rodeo Cowboys.

While him and Grandpa finished talking in the boot store.

Grandpa told Bo, "I know we talked about a few black cowboys that had their effect on the rodeo world. But black cowboys broke through some serious barriers to compete with everyone else."

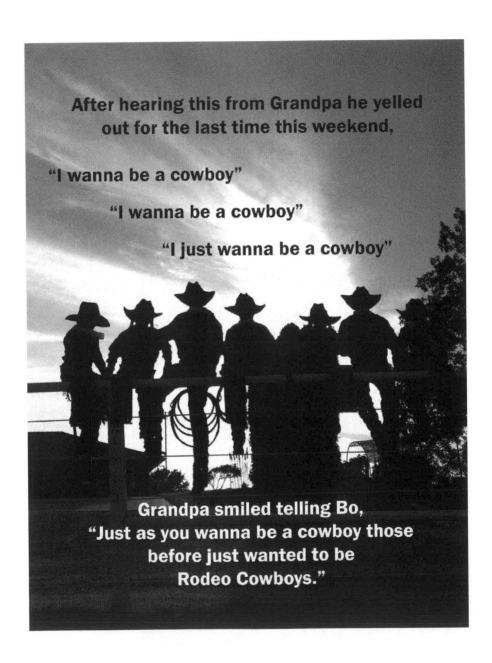

After hearing this from Grandpa he yelled
out for the last time this weekend,

"I wanna be a cowboy"

"I wanna be a cowboy"

"I just wanna be a cowboy"

Grandpa smiled telling Bo,
"Just as you wanna be a cowboy those
before just wanted to be
Rodeo Cowboys."

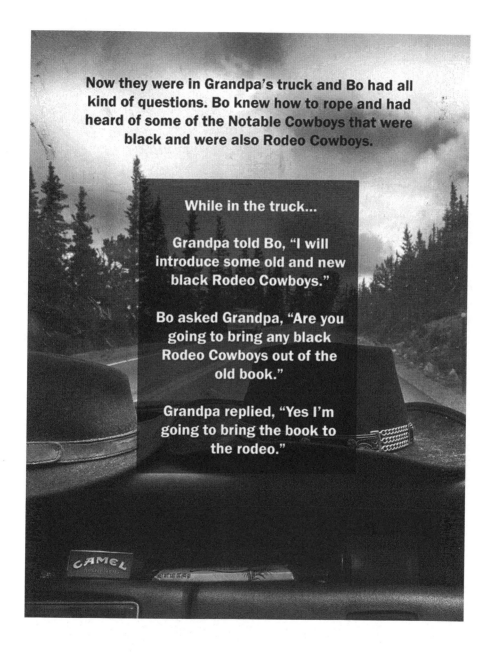

Now they were in Grandpa's truck and Bo had all kind of questions. Bo knew how to rope and had heard of some of the Notable Cowboys that were black and were also Rodeo Cowboys.

While in the truck...

Grandpa told Bo, "I will introduce some old and new black Rodeo Cowboys."

Bo asked Grandpa, "Are you going to bring any black Rodeo Cowboys out of the old book."

Grandpa replied, "Yes I'm going to bring the book to the rodeo."

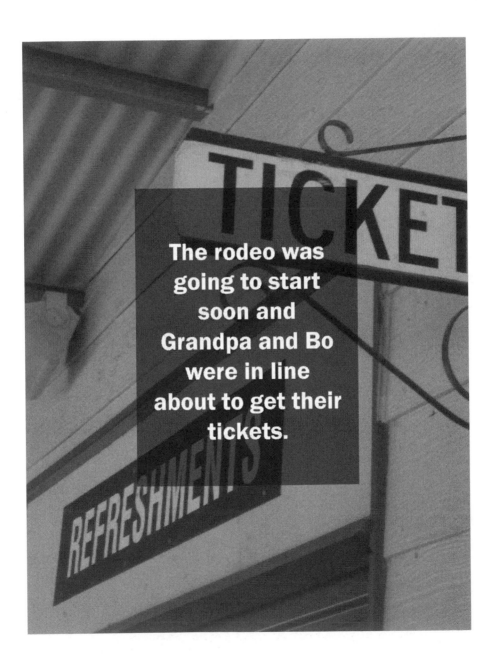

The rodeo was going to start soon and Grandpa and Bo were in line about to get their tickets.

Once the two of them had received their tickets, Bo was ready for the rodeo to begin.

All the cowboys from all over had come to the middle of the arena...

Now the rodeo was about to begin with the first event Bareback Bronco riding. Cowboys riding on a bronc that is attempting to throw or buck off the Rodeo Cowboy.

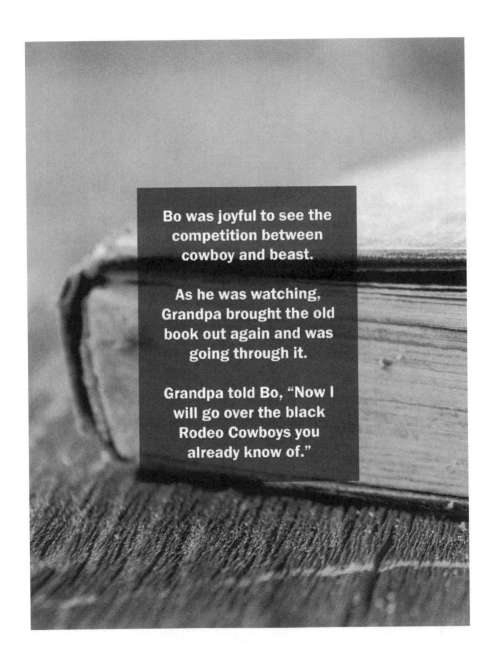

Bo was joyful to see the competition between cowboy and beast.

As he was watching, Grandpa brought the old book out again and was going through it.

Grandpa told Bo, "Now I will go over the black Rodeo Cowboys you already know of."

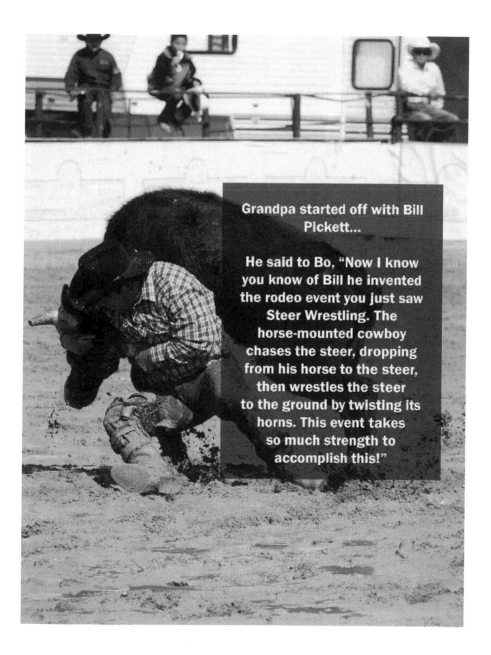

Grandpa started off with Bill Pickett...

He said to Bo, "Now I know you know of Bill he invented the rodeo event you just saw Steer Wrestling. The horse-mounted cowboy chases the steer, dropping from his horse to the steer, then wrestles the steer to the ground by twisting its horns. This event takes so much strength to accomplish this!"

The next event was Team Roping one of Bo's favorite events.

Grandpa brought up how Nate Love was one of the best Rodeo Cowboy ropers, winning many rodeos back in the day.

Now it was Saddle Bronco riding time...

Grandpa and Bo turned their attention to the bucking chutes.

Bo saw the cowboys getting ready to try and ride eight seconds.

While the rides were going on Grandpa flipped through the book and Jesse Stahl came up for his terrific rodeo skills.

Grandpa told Bo, "Remember Bo I told you about Jesse Stahl when I was talking about Notable Cowboys. Jesse was one tough Rodeo Cowboy, he faced discrimination in many rodeos because of his color. One rodeo he deserved first place for his ride but received second place because of color. The story goes, he rode a bucking bronco back facing backwards just to show off his skill."

Bo thought that was the coolest thing...

Now going away from the bucking chutes...

It was time for Calf-Roping!

Grandpa LeRoy brought up some major Rodeo Cowboys on the rodeo trail right now.

Bo asked, "Who are they Grandpa?"

Grandpa replied, "Fred Whitefield and Cory Solomon are some of the Calf Ropers right now."

Now it was time for Barrel Racing...

As the grounds crew was getting the arena ready, Bo was waiting

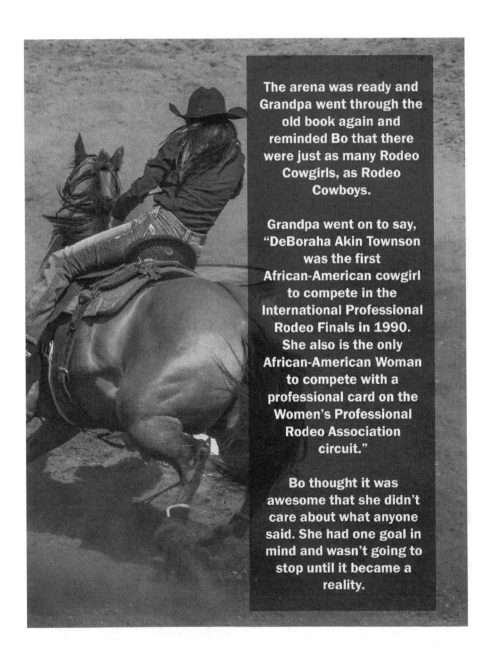

The arena was ready and Grandpa went through the old book again and reminded Bo that there were just as many Rodeo Cowgirls, as Rodeo Cowboys.

Grandpa went on to say, "DeBoraha Akin Townson was the first African-American cowgirl to compete in the International Professional Rodeo Finals in 1990. She also is the only African-American Woman to compete with a professional card on the Women's Professional Rodeo Association circuit."

Bo thought it was awesome that she didn't care about what anyone said. She had one goal in mind and wasn't going to stop until it became a reality.

Now Barrel Racing was over...

The grounds crew came out and took the barrels away and now it was time for some bucking bulls!

As some of the Rodeo Cowboys were riding their bucking bulls, Grandpa LeRoy looked through the book another time and found Charles Sampson.

Grandpa went on to say, "Charles in 1982 was the World Champion bull rider. He is the first black cowboy to win a World Title in the PRCA."

Now Grandpa and Bo were heading back to the truck...

Grandpa LeRoy was going to take his grandson Bo back to his parent's home.

While the two of them were traveling back...

Bo thought about everything he had learned this weekend.

Grandpa LeRoy asked Bo, "So what do you think about everything from this weekend?"

Bo replied, "Grandpa this was one of the best weekends I didn't realize there were so many black Rodeo Cowboys and Rodeo Cowgirls."

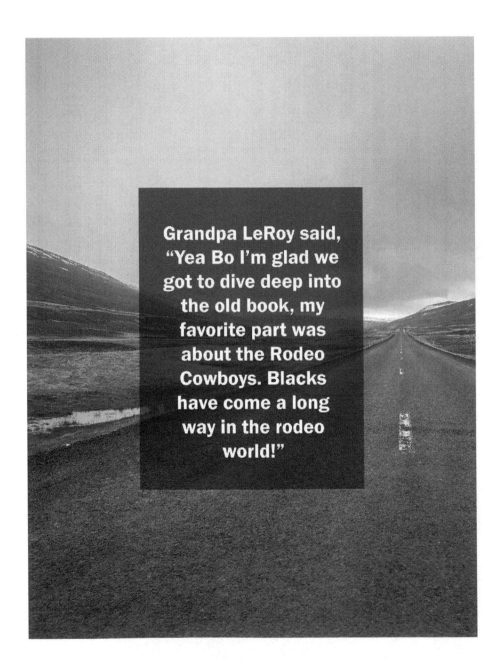

Grandpa LeRoy said, "Yea Bo I'm glad we got to dive deep into the old book, my favorite part was about the Rodeo Cowboys. Blacks have come a long way in the rodeo world!"

Grandpa also stated, "Bo never take for granted all the Black Rodeo Cowboys who came before you. From Cleo Hearn who founded the huge rodeo called Cowboys of Color, and many others like Jesse Stahl and Nate Love."

Bo sat back in the truck seat and looked out the window...

Bo knew they were getting close to his home...

As Grandpa LeRoy pulled down Bo's driveway towards the home, he smiled knowing that the information of Black Rodeo Cowboys was in good hands now!

Now both Bo and Grandpa went to the doorstep and Bo gave Grandpa LeRoy a hug goodbye.

Bo said to Grandpa, "Thanks for this weekend you're my favorite Cowboy of all time!"

Grandpa LeRoy replied, "No Bo you're my favorite new Cowboy."

As Grandpa was leaving the home the dust started to stir in the air.

Grandpa LeRoy shouted to Bo,

"Until next time partner!"

Author Bio

**Trae Q.L Venerable, born to Myron and Tracy
Venerable with a life long history in
ranching and farming, is excited to bring
you *Grandpa I Just Wanna be a Cowboy*,
books of the "forgotten cowboys" history.
Trae, an avid outdoorsman, horseman and
cattle jock, comes from generations of
Farm and Ranch owners, from which many
of these stories have been passed on. For
way too long, the "forgotten cowboy" has
not been heard and the time is now.**

**Visit his website at:
www.traevenerable.com**

On Sale Now!

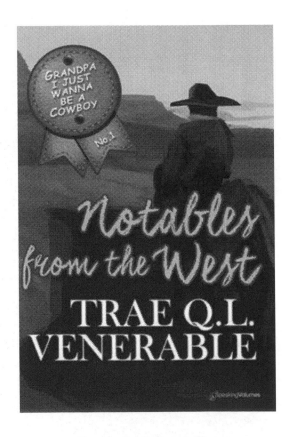

For more information
visit: www.speakingvolumes.us

Coming Soon!

Grandpa I Just Wanna be a Cowboy:
Women In the West

Made in the USA
Lexington, KY
25 April 2018